# Fairytale

## —A ROMANTIC DRAMA—

## Raquel McFarland

ISBN 979-8-9918295-0-2

Printed in the USA

# DEDICATION:

This is dedicated to all who have a dream and faithfully push through obstacles that get in the way of achieving that dream. Don't stop believing in yourself and never let anyone tell you that you can't. Always know that with God, you can!

Years in the making.....Finally!!!

# TABLE OF CONTENTS

# FOREWORD

In her debut book, My Fairytale (A Romantic Drama), Raquel McFarland surprises the reader with a genre mix of romance, drama, and suspense! Don't let the title fool you-it sounds like a sweet story of "happily ever after," but there are some twists and turns to getting there.

You might see yourself, a friend, a family member, or someone you used to know in one of the characters. In either case, as the plot builds and the suspense titillates, your imagination will be so excited it will be hard to put this book down.

If your curiosity is not heightened as you take in the first couple of chapters, keep reading and watch how you are so caught up that you reach the end before you realize it. This is a quick and delightful read that you will not only enjoy but will want everyone you know to read it as well.

Stephanie Duran

# Introduction

Meet Alexis…

He rode in on a white horse. Upper-torso exposed, displaying muscles I never knew could be formed on one man's body. White linen pants adorned his lower torso perfectly hanging on ever so slightly at the waist, leaving the imagination to wonder what was to follow. He smelled of the fresh ocean breeze, with his chest glistening from the sweat of his long journey. His bald head begged for me to caress it with my gentle hands in an effort to relieve his tension. He smiled brightly with the straightest, whitest, most perfect teeth ever. His masculine deep voice mesmerized me right out of my seat. My lips quivered as he spoke, "Hello, might you tell me where I can find a cool drink to quench my thirst?" He reached his hand out to gently lift me to my feet, where we met face to face. Our lips on the verge of touching as I answered, "Yes, right over there, at the bar. Allow me to lead you." As I turned, our hands intertwined…something hit me on my head.

"Girl, wake up, snap out of it," yelled Bonquisha.

"Oh, I guess I did it again. He was soooooo handsome and chocolate. Fine, girl, just fine!"

"One day you will meet this mystery man and when you do, I hope he has a brother, uncle, cousin... something, just as fine if not finer," she laughed.

"I know... Right? What do we have up for today? You feel like shopping, pigging out on some ice cream or catching a movie?"

"Girl, neither, you know I have a hot date with Raheim." Bonquisha replied.

"Oh...My...Goodness!.....No you did NOT just say Raheim??? That trifling...."

"Wait a minute now, watch your mouth! He may not be your fairytale, but he's all I got to work with right now. I don't see you doing any better with your dreamy imagination for a friend...," retorted Bonquisha as she entreats us to a pillow fight.

"Ow! That was my head. That's not funny! Take that." I swung with all the strength I could muster and pounded her back-to-back with every pillow in my path. I won, of course!

"I'm just saying. I am bored and you are always running off with Raheim and then you come right back running to me talking bad about him. I mean, if he's not all that and what you are looking for, why bother?"

"Well, I already told him we would go out. You need to get out more."

"And go where? What exactly is there to do out there? And who will I go with? It's not like I have a lot of options, you know."

"Exactly! How are you going to get any new options unless you get out there and explore? Expand your horizons, live a little! You always want to stay in the house and just be plain boring…"

"Okay, okay! That's enough! I get it. I'm still not going anywhere tonight with this hair looking like this and your Aunt Bertha is paying me a visit right now…."

"Ewww, T…M…I….!"

"Whatever! You just go have fun or whatever you do with Raheim…."

"Don't hate!"

Bonquisha left and went on her merry way to meet the 'fabulous' Raheim. He is so tired. I don't know what she sees in him. He never pays for anything and all he does is try to get her booty. I am so tired of the same old rap these so-called men of today try to dish out. They just want women who can do for themselves so they don't have to do anything or spend any money. I'm not saying it's all about the money, but still, a brother could open the door and pay sometimes. Whatever happened to chivalry? I know it's not dead and I know there are some mothers out there teaching these boys...I mean men...how to treat a lady. Maybe we as women need to learn how to be a real lady and not be so quick to give it up. So in essence, maybe it's our fault...no, I won't even go that route. But there are some trifling sisters out there too. They make it hard for us who are still good and holding out for Mr. Right, if there is such a thing.

I'm just saying, why can't I have all that I want in one person? Does that person not exist? God has to know what I need and has to be in the process of making and grooming him before sending him to me. Or maybe, God is grooming me, either way, this is agonizing, wanting someone and something that is so close but you just can't reach it no matter how hard you try. This is my life. Depressing almost, but I suppose it's all about timing and in His time it will come true.

God doesn't really need any help, but just to be sure, here is a synopsis of what I am looking for:

God fearing Christian man who is tall, handsome, my age or slightly older; it would help if he has not been married before and has no kids – I don't want someone who has been there, done that, but would rather go there together for the first time; He needs to be intelligent and business savvy; he needs to understand me and my needs; be a good help around the house for the things a man ought to do; be appreciative of all I am giving and do and willing to give back just as much; like to have fun and sometimes be spontaneous; strong, gentle and kind; sexy and knows what to do in the bedroom, knows how to communicate, is truthful and faithful….

Okay, I think I am getting too detailed and a bit off track, but you have to be careful of what you ask, you just might get it!

I've been told that I need to keep my head out of the clouds, but that is the only place I seem to get peace. It's very calming and soothing; allows me to do what I do best, daydream about my fairytale I hope to come true.

# WHO'S THAT GUY

Ring, ring...

"ehlo?" I answered with a raspy voice.

"Wake up sleepy head! Get up and wash your stanking breath!" yelled Bonquisha from the other end of the line.

"Whatever! Yours smells worse than mine, I'm sure, since you were all kissy-faced with Raheim.... uuhhh!"

"Girl, I have got to tell you about my night!"

"Oh Lord!" What happened now?" I sighed as I sat up in bed, rubbing my eyes and yawning. I knew I was about to get an earful.

"No, this is good! Great news for you!!"

"For me? How so?" I was a bit curious as to what she was talking about. I couldn't imagine how it would be good..."great" news for me...After looking at the phone with a crazy smirk, shrugging my shoulders and shaking my head, I hopped up and ran downstairs to start the coffee. I loved the smell of coffee, before, during and after brewing. It is so inviting.

"Hush and let me tell you, dang!!!!"

"Now you know that was too close…."

"What? I said dang!" Bonquisha shouted with a bit of disturbance in her voice. She only talked with such a high pitch when I was starting to work her nerves...I always get a kick out of upsetting her. It is soooooo funny!!!

"I know! That's what I'm talking about." I said.

"Oh Lord, can I just tell you…"

"Don't be using the Lord's name in vain!", I cut her off.

"You just said it!... Look, we are getting off track. Shush so I can tell you the good news…"

"Yeah, whatever, I am so sure.."

"You ready for this?" Bonquisha said with impatience.

"Yes, now spit it out! You have already wasted my good extra fifteen minutes of sleep I was trying to get. What is soooo good…great???"

"Well, as you know, I went out with Raheim last night…"

"Yeah, gross…what else is new?" I ventured from the bedroom to the kitchen. Coffee, must have coffee…Columbian flavor will do for today. After brewing, I began to pour my coffee into my favorite coffee cup and generously add sugar. Hmmmm, which cream should I add today, hazelnut or french vanilla??? I'll add both I thought as I drifted off in thought not really listening to Bonquisha rant and rave about her night. All of a sudden, I felt the splatter of hot coffee bouncing from the floor onto my fluffy pink slippers and my foot. My mouth opened wide, I shouted, "What did you just say?"

"What? Were you not listening to me? Did you hear anything I just said?" Bonquisha asked.

"Obviously not! Repeat the part after you and Raheim left the restaurant where YOU paid for the meal AND drinks and then went to The Spot…"

The Spot is, or should I say was, a nice place to hang out with your friends, get your groove on and have a few beverages. That was until the shootout and new management took over. It seems like they don't really care about the place and all they are after is the money. No one wants to go to a run down, hole in the wall with bullets lodged in the walls. YES, the bullets are still there!!! Nevertheless, it was still packed every weekend, with a new breed of party goers.

"Smarty pants! So you were listening!"

"Yes, now start from there, you have my full attention!" I urged.

"You should have been listening the first time, wench!" Bonquisha yelled.

"Will you just get on with it....man!" I screamed playfully.

"Well, as I was saying, we went to The Spot. Everybody was looking fly. You had the big girls in one corner, the skinny girls in the other, and all the cool people in the middle or in the VIP section. Of course, Raheim and I were in VIP with his boys and a few chicks I hadn't met before."

While Bonquisha rambled, I thought to myself I am so sure she paid for VIP too! At least Raheim stayed constant; his boys always had a new face every time.

"Well, we were making our way to the dance floor and this guy I had never seen before pulled me by the arm like he didn't see Raheim all wrapped around me. I was like, OH NO! What did he do that for???"

I would have been worried too! Raheim has a temper. No one touches his woman, no one!!! Word on the street is he shot someone and stabbed someone else. That is also why I wondered how she could be with him. He must be doing something right, but only God knows what! But I couldn't help but laugh as I heard the concern in her voice. Bonquisha is soooooooo dramatic!! But at least she keeps it real for me.

"Raheim turned around and all I know was the guy was laid out on the floor! We continued to the dance floor without missing a beat. It seemed like no one even noticed. I was wrong!!! Three dudes rolled up on Raheim with guns drawn! I started screaming."

Now, as she is telling me this story, I'm thinking, what part of this is great for me? Like, can she hurry up and get to the good, great part already???

"Raheim's boys surrounded the three dudes with even bigger guns and everybody ran out of there, including security! Words were exchanged and the three guys backed down. As it turned out, the guy that pulled my arm just wanted to get at me so he could get at you!"

"Okay, this is where I spilled the coffee on my brand new pink fluffy slippers, thank you!!!" I said with sarcasm, letting her know she was buying me some more slippers on our next shopping trip. "What do you mean he was trying to get at you so he could get at me? Do I know him? How exactly does he know me? And, if you never saw him before, then how would he know you and I are connected? What is really going on?"

"Uhm, can I finish the story please?" Bonquisha asked, and I know she was looking at me all twisted through the phone but I didn't care. I had questions and she wasn't answering them fast enough!

"YES, Duuhhh...hurry it along....the suspense is killing me." I replied.

"So, of course, the club closed early for the night. The guys sat and had drinks for about an hour. I was the only female in there besides the two bartenders that stayed. The police came, and all too late, but they came and everything was cool by then. See, you can't never trust the police to be there when you need them...."

"Uh, Bonquisha? You're getting off track!"

"Oh! So, the guy told Raheim that he was a friend of his cousin Pookie. He met Pookie at the party for Grandpa Brooks' 65th birthday in May. Grandpa Brooks is Raheim's dad. You remember that night, right?"

"Yeah...." I said with hesitation as I try to scan my memory of the faces that were at the party and the people hanging around Pookie. You can't miss Pookie with his slicked back long permed hair and his hazel eyes. He drives a big, fuchsia Chevy

Avalanche truck, all decked out and fully loaded, with chrome everything and bass you can hear about 10 miles away it seems.

"Well, he…"

"What is "his" name?" I interrupted.

"Oh, he said he goes by KB."

"Interesting."

"Yeah, I thought so too." She continued. "So KB went on babbling about how he met Pookie and how they've been tight ever since. He then said that he saw Raheim and me with one beautiful girl that seemed to cling to us like white on rice. She seemed a bit shy, he said, and he just knew he had to get to know her."

"Cling? White on rice? WHATEVER!!!!" I said, while rolling my neck and eyes as if she could see me.

"Well, you were a bit clingy, especially since it was just before the one-year anniversary of when your father got shot." Bonquisha reminded me.

"Okay, carry on with the story. I don't want to start tearing up. You know that is still a sore subject for me even though it has been over a year since it happened."

My dad and I were really close. I really loved him. He was a decorated cop in the Miami police force and was shot in the line of duty by none other than a drug dealer! It was a sting operation and he was first to barge in. A stray bullet hit him in the side and went right through his body hitting both lungs. It was a tragic day as I had just received my Ph.D. and was on my way to tell him. I had planned a celebration dinner that night. He was a good man and didn't deserve to die that way. I really miss him.

"Raheim called me over and asked your name. Girl, you know he has a bad memory when it comes to names. It took him three weeks to remember mine. I was "Baby" for the longest!" She laughed; however, I didn't think it was funny.

"I told him your name and he politely sent me away. Girl, I was like, how rude!!! But he slipped me a bill in the process so, I was like cool...Anyway...They talked for about another half hour and as we were leaving KB asked me for your number."

"You didn't give it to him, did you?"

"Girl, YES! He is fine! Almost fits the description of your mystery man. If I wasn't with Raheim, I would try to get with him. I might still try...."

"Oh Lord, help us!" I screamed.

"What?" Bonquisha screamed back. I just knew she had a twisted look on her face. I had to laugh even though I was serious.

"How can you just give out my number and you didn't even ask me? I don't know this dude! You don't either! He could be a murderer for all I know, a drug dealer, a serial killer psycho...I don't like this! I don't like it one bit! And who goes through all this kind of trouble just to meet a girl, especially little ole me? He must be really desperate, especially if he is as fine as you say he is...."

"Do you hear yourself, Alexis?" Bonquisha asked.

"What?

"You must not realize how beautiful you truly are. I aspire to be more like you everyday. You don't even have to try very hard, except you should comb your hair more often, but other than that, you are truly beautiful inside and out! Why wouldn't a guy want to go through all that trouble? He saw in you what you obviously don't see in yourself and he wants it! Celebrate it, girl, celebrate your beauty!" Bonquisha encouraged.

As ghetto as I thought she was, she always seemed to find a way to encourage me. That is why she is my BFF for life! I don't know where I would be without her.

"Well, thanks, but I will have to think about it."

"You do that!"

We hung up the phone. As I leaned over the counter while finishing my coffee, I noticed a smile coming over my face. Wow, that was the first time I have smiled like that in a long while...probably since I last saw and talked to my dad. Maybe this IS good...GREAT...for me....maybe....

# THE CALL

A week has passed and I still haven't received the call. If Mr. KB was so interested, why hasn't he called me yet? I really didn't care at first, but now curiosity has me on edge! He's probably doing this on purpose. Yep, this is part of his game plan. All men do it and they think it gives them the upper hand when really all it does is irritate women. If you are sooooo interested, why play games? Who has time for games?

Wait a minute...why am I tripping? I don't even know this dude. He has some nerve trying to get at me like that. I wonder what his real motive is and why me? Hmmm...well, unless he calls me I guess I will never find out....there I go again. I need to do something to occupy my mind. Looks like pampering time!

I went into my beautiful master bath with a huge Jacuzzi tub and started the water. Ahhh...nice and hot, just like I like it. Add a little lavender and chamomile and some fresh rose petals, purple roses no doubt. Light a few aroma therapy candles. Pour a nice glass of Moscato....oh, yeah, this is the life.

My dad left me this big mansion when he died. I had already helped him decorate it so there was not much to change once I moved in. The master bath was my favorite part of the entire house. I could sit in here for hours and never come out.

Just as I finished running my bath water and was about to get in, to my surprise the phone rings. Of all times to ring, why did it have to ring now? Man, can't enjoy nuthin!

"Hello?" I answered with much attitude.

"Oh, I'm sorry. Did I catch you at a bad time?" The smooth sounding voice cooed on the other end.

"Well, not really. It depends on who this is." I retorted slyly. I knew good and well who it was. No guys ever called me except my dad. And he didn't sound anything like my dad, especially since he was no longer alive. No, this mystery man had a sexy seductive deep voice. He actually called just in time. I might enjoy my bath even more just listening to his smooth deep voice. Hope I don't fall asleep....

"Well, you don't know me but I go by KB. I saw you about six months ago at a party." He continued.

"I don't go to parties. Are you sure it was me you saw?" I interrupted, knowing good and well I was at that very party that he was talking about. But I didn't see him there so I have no proof he was there and I didn't want him to know that I knew anything or was waiting on his call. He chuckled and continued to feed me his story.

"A partner of mine told me about the party. He mentioned there would be some hot and sexy babes there. Some of Miami's finest. So I went."

Oh so he was looking for a hot sexy babe? Wow, that is so not me. I knew he was desperate!!

"Oh, well, I know I wasn't there then." I interjected.

"Why would you say that?" He asked curiously.

"I am no where near hot and sexy, nor a babe, nor one of Miami's finest!" I laughed.

"Have you seen yourself? You shouldn't be so hard on yourself. You obviously don't see what I saw that night."

"And what exactly is it that you saw on this night that I was supposedly out partying with Miami's finest?" I was having way too much fun with this. I can't remember the last time I had this much fun. It was almost getting to be too much fun and I didn't want to jump the gun like I always do. I decided I would take this real slow and feel everything out before I allow my feelings to overtake my wisdom.

"Since you asked, I will tell you." He began. "I saw a beautiful 5'8" caramel brown skin voluptuous woman with silky long hair. I saw a woman who appeared confident yet needy…and by that I mean a woman needing a man to sweep her off her feet and take care of her in all the ways a man should. Then I saw that man as me and I knew I had to have you."

Oh my goodness, no he didn't! How could he possibly feed me such weak and lame garbage? Is he serious? He is definitely not from around here! And what exactly does he mean needy? He better be lucky he explained himself and I can't literally come through the phone on his behind!

"Uhm, KB, not to cut you off, but if you truly saw all of that, why did it take you six whole months to find me? Why didn't you try to talk to me that night? I am finding this very hard to believe."

"Well Dear,..."

Dear? Where does he get off calling me Dear? He doesn't know me well enough to call me Dear. That's like married couple terminology or a couple that has been dating for quite some time…uhhhh, he is so lame and out of touch. How could Bonquisha do this to me? Someone needs to help him with his game, I thought to myself as I quietly laughed at his efforts to woo me. He was so unsuccessful at this point. So far, the only thing he had going for him was his voice, that late night, quiet storm kind of voice.

"Perfection takes time and you can't rush a good thing. I like to let things marinate and if it sits there long enough, it will be just right when you are ready to divulge."

Okay, now I am laughing uncontrollably to myself… He just can't be serious. Where does he get this stuff? Out of magazines? I quietly listened and laughed while he continued to ramble…

"And by the way, you just admitted you were at the party!" He thought he had caught me, but I am too clever for that.

"I did not! I said no such thing. All I said was IF you saw me that night why didn't you talk to me that night? I never once indicated I was there. Thank you!"

"Okay, okay, you win! You don't have to throw in the attitude. I like to keep things nice and pleasant. I am a peaceful kind of man and don't like too much drama." He said.

That's not what I heard. According to Bonquisha, he started a whole bunch of mess and almost got himself killed behind it. He should really be more careful and know who he is dealing with before making any kind of approach, especially in a club where everyone has been drinking and is fully inebriated.

"SO, Mr. KB. Tell me more about you. What does KB stand for? What do you do? Have you been married? Do you have any kids? Where are you from? What do you do for fun? What are you looking for in a mate? Are you looking to settle down? Do you even want kids or more kids?"

"Whoa!!! Slow down, lil' mama!!" he shouted over my interrogation session. "Let me answer one question at a time."

"Okay, shoot! I'm all ears!" I hope I didn't sound too eager.

"Well, I don't usually tell people my name. Not that I am not proud of it but I just like to keep it simple. So, KB it is. In due time, you will come to know my full name. Right now, I am between jobs as I just moved here earlier this year from Pittsburgh, and the job I had closed down a couple of months ago. I have never been married nor do I have any kids. Yes, I would like to settle down soon and eventually have 2 or 3 children. How about you?" He asked.

"I thought you knew everything about me the way you were talking earlier." I said, laughing.

"Well, I know enough. But, I would like to hear it from the horse's mouth."

The horse's mouth?  Really???  That is your response?  "So now I'm a horse?"

"Noooo, you know what I mean.  I want to hear it from you not by word of mouth."

"Uh huh…Well, I am from Miami.  I don't have kids and have never been married. Waiting on Mr. Right, if there is such a thing."

"That would be me!" He retorted.

"Excuse me?" I knew what he said; I just had to ask to make sure.

"You heard me. I don't nor did I stutter. You might want to get some of that wax out of your ears." He laughed.

"Well, Mr. Smarty Pants! We will just have to see about that!" I shot back.

"Yes, we will, over dinner! Tomorrow night. I will pick you up at 7 pm.  Be ready!" Click.

No he didn't! He didn't give me a chance to say yes or no. He didn't ask for my address or nothing.  I bet that trifling Bonquisha gave him ALL my info! I am going to get her! She conveniently left that tidbit of information out of her story. Hmmm, I wonder what else she told him.  Let me call her right now....

# GETTING READY

"Now remember, don't be too eager. Remember what I taught you!"

"Bonquisha! I know what to do."

"Yeah, but you know how you are! You tend to go left and next thing you know, you are over the cliff and crying on my shoulder the next day….swearing men off for the rest of your life."

"Whatever!" I sneered.

"You know that is the truth. Remember Stephen? You were head over hills in love with him after three months. Then you found out he was cheating on you the whole time. You might oughta give up the good girl celibacy stance…"

"Nope! I won't and Stephen doesn't even count!"

"Uh huh….whatever, Alexis! Now, what are you going to wear?"

"Girl, you know I don't know! I never know until the last minute and even then I change about 3 or 4 times before I finally settle on something."

"Well, you can't wait until 7 pm. You need to figure it out now. You need me to come over? Yep, I am on the way!" Bonquisha hung up the phone.

What is it with everyone hanging up on me? No one has any manners these days. Last I checked, you don't just hang up on a person, you say "good bye" first then hang up....my thoughts were interrupted by a loud banging on the door and repeated ringing of the doorbell. Couldn't be anybody but Bonquisha!

I ran to the door and looked through the peephole. Why did I see the little bad kids from down the street outside my door? What could they possibly want this time?

"What?!" I screamed through the door.

"We need to come in. We are scared." They screamed.

"Scared of what?" I already knew that their mother and father had to be arguing again. They always run to my house when that happens, just until things cooled down. And their mother would come down and get them, shirt torn, bruises forming, black eyes and all. When are they ever going to get it?

"Call the police and go back home! I can't help you right now." I felt bad but I had a date to get ready for and this was going to set me back. The way they were banging on the door, it seemed like this one was going to be another all-nighter. I think they do it on purpose to have a free babysitter and get some quality time in …..you know, "make up sessions"… that's how they got so many kids in the first place! I might have to start charging. I looked back out the peephole and they were gone. This time, I heard the mother shouting at the father as he was driving off. Good! I was not in the mood for that. I know I sound selfish, but this date was far too important to let neighborhood drama ruin it! There was too much at stake and I wanted everything to be perfect.

Ding, Ding…..there goes the doorbell again. That better be Bonquisha, and if it is, I am surprised at how quickly she got here! She always took so long for anything, don't matter what it is. She believes in making everybody wait for her. Me, her mom, her man of the week….didn't matter.

"Hey girl! Now, let's get to that closet!" She said as she barged through the door.

"What's in the bags?" I asked.

"I brought a few extra things in case I didn't like what you have, and usually I don't." she retorted.

I rolled my eyes at her. She has some nerve! "Well, why even waste time going through my closet? Let's see what you got in the bag. NOW!" I yelled and laughed.

"Whoa, hold your horses, perfection takes patience. You of all people should know that, as much of a perfectionist as you are!"

What is with the reference to horses? Am I fat or what? I know I need to lose a few pounds but geez!!!

I grabbed the bag from her hand and dumped the contents on my bed. She looked at me like I was crazy, but I didn't care. Hmmm, purple! She knows me too well! Purple is my favorite color although you wouldn't be able to tell. There is very little of it in my closet. I began rummaging through the clothes and accessories she brought. She thinks of everything! There were matching purses and shoes in the bag. Good thing we wear the same size! Most of the clothes still had the tags on them. Bonquisha shops like there is no tomorrow! Over half of the clothes in her closet have tags still on them.

"Here, try this one on." She said impatiently. "Time is ticking."

It was a purple jumpsuit with spaghetti straps and ballooned out on the legs stopping around the bottom of the calves. To it she added a gold belt, huge gold hoop earrings, and gold shoes. I twirled around in the mirror for about 5 minutes after putting the entire ensemble on and decided, no, this is not it.

"Okay, try this!"

This one was really nice. It was a purple top with one shoulder exposed. Again, there was gold involved, notice a theme here? I added a new pair of dark blue jeans that just so happened to have gold bedazzle on the back pockets. And the same gold shoes completed the look. I liked this one, but no, it wasn't calling my name just yet.

"This is the last outfit my dear, then we will have to pull a miracle out of your closet!" Bonquisha laughed.

"Not Funny! I have some nice stuff. You are just jazzier than I am." I snatched the outfit out of her hands and put it on. Added the accessories and shoes, and voila! Beautiful! This was the one. It was a purple spaghetti strap dress that flared out in the fashion of an A-line dress, accentuating my curves. The accessories were gold of course – gold belt, gold and purple infused bracelet, my favorite gold watch, and gold dangly earrings. The same gold shoes I tried on with the previous outfits and a small purple clutch lined in gold with a flower in the middle.

"You are right! It is perfect! I knew you needed my help." She teased. "Now, let's fix that hair. What time is it?"

"It is 6 pm! You better hurry. I want to be ready when he gets here." I said.

"Well, I have already worked a miracle with your clothes. Let me see what I can do with this mess on your head!"

My hair was straight. I had just washed and blow dried it this morning. She plugged up all the flat irons she had and pulled out a bunch of different stuff to put in my hair to make it hold. It looked like she was about to perform surgery! After about forty minutes of straightening, curling, pinning, and spraying, etc, she was finally done.

"Wonderful! This is why you are my friend. Okay, not the only reason, but you know what I mean. Thanks Bonquisha." I began to admire myself in the mirror. She had my hair pulled back in a ponytail with individual curls hanging and a small amount of hair swooped across my forehead for a bang. A few curls playfully hung loosely out of the ponytail in the back to ever so slightly drape my neck. She used enough sprays to make it shiny, glittery, and hold just right.

"Uhm, Alexis?"

"Yes?" I replied, wondering what was wrong.

"I know you not going like that?"

"Like what?" I asked.

"Bare-faced!"

"You know I am so natural." I blew her off.

"Yeah, but not tonight!" She began applying dark brown eyeliner, a couple of light eye colors and followed it with a purplish eye color. A little bit of mascara and then lips! "Perfect!" she screamed.

Ding Ding.... I must get that doorbell sound changed I thought as Bonquisha ran to the door. With my heart racing, I took a deep breath and stood patiently in the living room smiling to hide my nervousness. He's here! Okay, breathe, relax, breathe...stop sweating under arms...stop bubbling stomach...breathe.... you would think I was having a baby or something. Alright, I'm good, I think. I winked at Bonquisha as we walked out of the door toward an evening of what I hoped would be pure fun and elegance.

# FIRST DATE

"This place is great." I leaned over to whisper in his ear.

"Have you ever been here before?" KB asked.

"No, but I had heard about it." I replied.

He picked me up in a black Lamborghini and we practically flew to the restaurant. You couldn't really feel how fast we were going; it was a smooth ride. The restaurant was a popular place across town, Benny's of Miami. I had always heard about it and wanted to go there but never got the chance. It's an upscale place with a huge dance floor and live bands. Good choice on his part....

"So, do you like it?" he asked.

"Yes, it is very nice." I replied. I could feel myself blushing. I hadn't been on a date in quite some time and this isn't bad for my first date in a while. KB is awfully handsome. I can see why Bonquisha gave him my number. He truly resembles the guy in my daydreams. He is tall, handsome, and I can even see his muscles through his shirt. Dressed to a tee with a fresh haircut and shave, I had to catch myself from drooling.

"What? ... Oh, yes, I am ready to order. What do you recommend?" I asked. Somehow, I had drifted off in my own thoughts and didn't hear him ask if I was ready to eat. Okay, get a grip, compose yourself! Never let him see you sweat...I am trying to motivate myself here to not be so eager.... I hope he can't tell how mesmerized I am...

"Well, the salmon is pretty good or the shrimp. And by the way you look stunning! Even better than when I first saw you." He whispered in my ear sending chills right down my spine. He better be careful, there is a lot bottled up inside just waiting to come out and I don't think he's ready for it....

"Hmmmm, I think I will go with the salmon and a salad."

The waiter came over and just as a gentleman should, KB ordered both my meal and his along with a bottle of Moscato. How did he know? I guess it is becoming more popular now. Ever since I first started drinking Moscato, it seems like everyone jumped on the band wagon! Can't have nuthin' without everyone else trying to be like me.... I chuckled to myself.

The band was awesome. Their music crooned ever so smoothly and the crowd seemed to thoroughly enjoy it. I noticed I had begun to sway when KB leaned over and asked me to dance. This purple dress was about to get a workout! I could feel myself smiling real hard.... shake it off, control yourself... This is too much for me!

Wow, he can really dance. He is swinging me around with such grace and precision. Good thing I took dance lessons. Daddy would have it no other way. He wanted to make sure I was well-rounded and prepared for the husband God would bring me.

"You are a natural." KB whispered in my ear.

"Thanks. Not too bad yourself." I replied with my lips barely touching his earlobe. He better stop starting stuff! I am really trying here!

"Oh, look, the wine is ready and here comes the waiter with the food. Let's eat."

He grabbed my hand and guided us back toward the table. I was starving. I just then realized I hadn't eaten all day. Butterflies filled my stomach all day as I was nervously preparing for this date not knowing what to expect.

"How's your salmon?" KB asked.

"Great. How's your steak and shrimp?"

"Delicious, as usual." He replied.

"Oh, so you come here often? This is where you bring all your ladies?"

"No, I don't mean it like that. I just meant…"

"Uh huh, I know what you meant. You already said it." I cut him off and rolled my eyes. Here we go!

"Alexis."

He just had to say my name like that. Puppy dog eyes never worked on me before, but he had a way with them. How could I resist. And the way my name rolled off of his tongue followed by those big juicy lips…. Lord, please be with me!

"YES, KB?" I replied, trying to sound annoyed.

"I only accept the best. It is my pleasure to shop around for the best places to entertain the most beautiful woman I have ever met." He smiled, and leaned over to caress my face with his hand.

"Am I blushing?" I asked, embarrassed. There he goes with that lame stuff again. He really thinks I am going to fall for it. I will play his game and let him think it is working. It might very well be...but he will never know...must keep my cool....

We continued to eat dinner while listening to the band play all my favorites. How did they know? I could barely eat for dancing in my seat and trying to sing. The Moscato was working. I felt myself feeling totally relaxed with KB. There was a good vibe and I could tell he had a good heart. He seemed like such a beautiful man, inside and out.

"Care for dessert?" KB asked.

"Yes..."

"Good, guess we should get going." He cut me off.

"What do you mean?"

"Well, you said you wanted dessert and they didn't put me on the menu." He laughed.

"Cute, real cute!" I smirked. "You always have jokes."

"Gotta live life to the fullest and have fun." He replied.

"Well, I did have my eyes on the chocolate cake." But before I could finish my request, the waiter was already on the way to the table with a small platter of chocolate covered strawberries, pineapples, and bite size pieces of chocolate cake with chocolate icing. This cannot be real! How did he know? This night is going too perfect. Bonquisha!

We shared dessert and it was most delicious as I love chocolate. That's my middle name. Okay, not really, but it should be. He fed me bite after bite with sips of wine in between, here and there. I even returned the favor a couple of times. It was fun. We laughed and teased each other for the rest of the evening. A few more shakes on the dance floor and it was time to call it a night. Anymore sips of

Moscato and it would be a wrap! He would have to carry me out of here.

The valet brought the car around, smiling like he just got back from the joyride we both know he took while we dined. KB helped me get in the car and off we flew back to my place. I was a bit nervous. Do I invite him in? That would not be a good thing right now given the vulnerable state I am in. I'll just play it by ear and see what he does.

"Okay, Ms. Alexis. Here you are." He helped me to the door. "I enjoyed the first of many dates to come. You have a good night." He leaned in and gently kissed me on the cheek, turned and walked to his car, got in and drove off into the night. Wow, a true gentleman. I am impressed, very much so!

I closed the door behind me and melted onto the floor, startled by the ringing of my cell phone. It was him.

"Miss me already?" I asked playfully.

"Of course! One second of not being by your side is too much." He replied.

Cheesy! He is so cheesy, but I like it! I am blushing all the way upstairs to the bedroom. We talked until the wee hours of the morning, not missing a beat. It was 4 a.m. before I realized I needed some sleep if I planned on making it to church in the morning. What a wonderful evening, absolutely wonderful!

# HIS THOUGHTS

Drifting in and out of sleep, KB tosses and turns because of his thoughts of Alexis…. She is a really sweet girl. I think things may work out between us. It saddens me to know that my reasoning for contacting her caused her so much pain and could possibly cause more after it's all said and done. I have got to be careful with this. Being around her and talking to her makes me lose focus. This isn't supposed to happen to me. I was trained by the best to be the best, but I can't shake this overall feeling I have for her. Maybe I should ask the captain to pull me from the case, but there is no one who has gotten closer than I am right now.

Alexis is everything I am looking for in a woman. She is fine, witty, quick on her feet, and the most beautiful person I have ever met, inside and out. Devoted to church and very spiritual. She even spends most of her time volunteering at The Place for Refuge with children who have lost one or both of their parents. Although Alexis was an adult when she lost her father, she never knew her mother as she died giving birth. Her father never remarried.

He truly loved her mother and devoted his life to her and serving the community through his police work. I hope once she finds out what my initial intentions were that she doesn't abandon me. This job means as much to me as her father did to her. I heard many stories of how he worked the streets of Miami and put fear in anyone who dared to try him. He made it look so effortless, everyone would say. When she finds out who was really behind his death maybe that will redeem me.

We had such a good time. I could definitely see myself spending the rest of my life with her. Promises were made and I must keep them. Letting her father down now would not be honorable. Let me get my head together, go for a run. It's a perfect morning for it. Then I can deal with the scum of the earth, Raheim. It's time to put my plan into action.

After returning from his run, KB hears the phone ring as he is getting out of the shower.

Captain. He always knows when to call. It's like he has a sick sense for when I might be falling off the wagon and getting ready to slip up…

"Hey Captain…. Yes, everything is going according to plan. I have gained access to the target and his camp. It won't be long now…. Yes, I'm staying focused…I have everything under control."

If Captain finds out I have fallen for Alexis, he is going to have my hide! He knows me too well. The last time this happened, things didn't go in my favor. I need to come up with a real plan on getting this scum off the streets without losing the possible love of my life. But will she have me once she knows?

# Raheim

Man, Bonquisha knows how to keep me straight. I might just have to marry this one. She hood enough to hold me down, she understands me and she has style and class. What more could a guy ask for. Guess I should treat her right. She has been down with me for a while now, the only one to last this long. See, this is part of my process to weed out the weak. I need a strong woman by my side. Bonquisha is the one!

"Man, you gotta get with this cat! He is the real deal." said Pookie, interrupting Raheim's thoughts.

"Why? What makes him such the real deal? What's he talking about? And how you say you know him again?" asked Raheim.

"At Grandpa Brooks birthday party. He just showed up, new in town. Man, we kick it, he talking good game! You gotta get with him!" Pookie swore.

"New in town? You want me to mess with a new cat that's new to the set that none of us know from Timbuktu?" asked Raheim. "Are you crazy? Do you even know anything about him? The way he approached me at the club was not cool! And all that just to get with a girl he only saw once? That was lame and I don't trust it. You gotta come with more than that Pookie! Man, com'on, You not on your game and we don't have time for mistakes. Things just started to cool down." Raheim preached to Pookie.

Raheim was concerned. Hands shaking, he tried to take a sip of his drink and a puff of his cigarette.

"Yeah, man whatever! I'm telling you, it's cool!" Pookie reassured.

"You ready? Let's roll." Raheim said as they got ready to get in the wind. "Gotta make that paper, it's not going to make itself!"

"Yeah, I hear ya' but I'm on E, can't be your chauffer today." Laughed Pookie.

"When are you not on E? You need to stop running around with these crazy women. They only want your money and the way you flaunting it is drawing too much attention. You always gotta be flashy. What's up with that?" Raheim laughed back.

"Man, don't hate! I can't be no one woman man! I guts to have plenty of women around me! I'm not like you, all married up!" Pookie joked.

"Are you serious? You gon' come at me like that? Don't disrepects my woman! I'll put one in you right now!" Raheim got serious.

"Oh, you are serious about this one.... I see ya', I see ya'! You ain't gotta be tryin' to kill me!" Pookie tried to ease the situation. He knew how hot-headed his cousin could be, especially when he meant business about something.

"Bonquisha is real! I plan to pop the question soon." Raheim said.

"What???? Real????" Pookie asked, in shock.

"Yeah, man. She don't know so don't say nothing." Raheim warned.

"You got the ring yet? I know it's fat!" said Pookie.

"That's where we on the way to now." Raheim replied.

Not knowing what was to come, Raheim wanted to seal the deal with Bonquisha. He knew he was on borrowed time with her since he hadn't really showed her how he was raised to treat a lady. The streets had taken over and running around with all these women who just wanted his money and status had Raheim drained. He had to make sure Bonquisha was in it for the long haul and not just for the money. She never pressures him and is more than willing to take care of him at a drop of a dime without question.

"Yep, she's the one! Any other woman would have been long gone. It's been almost a year. I guess that's long enough to make her suffer. She deserves all this…" Raheim said out loud as his thoughts were taking over.

"What?" Pookie asked.

"Oh, nothing man." Raheim replied, startled. Man, I'm a G! I'm tripping! She got me daydreaming, Raheim thought to himself.

"Man, pull up over there. I need to check and collect on these fools!"

Pookie pulled over in the parking lot of the neighborhood corner store. Workers for Raheim would always get caught just standing around and he constantly had to check them. Collection was almost an hourly thing with them too. If he didn't collect as often as he did, they would pocket money and product.

"Man, I need to get rid of some of these cats. Maybe I will talk to yo' boy. I need some new, more careful blood." Raheim told Pookie.

Before Pookie could respond, Raheim was already out of the truck and had a piece to the temple of a dude trying to run game on him for his money. Pookie jumped out, ran up behind the dude with his piece drawn, backing up his cousin. All the other workers got scared and ran. They knew Raheim didn't play and being a witness meant a bullet in their temple too.

"That's right, run! I own these streets and ya'll betta respect me! I got the cops scared and eating out of the palms of my hands! How you gon' try to run game on me? Where my money?! Where my money?!" Raheim was shouting.

"Get in the truck!" Raheim shouted. He knew it was too hot to shoot the dude in the street so he had to take him somewhere else and then dump the body.

Pookie was always afraid of Raheim when he would go into a rage and want to shoot up everything. That's the nature of the business and Pookie knew it had to be that way. But why today? Why couldn't this have happened on another day when Raheim was riding with one of his other boys? Pookie was thinking to himself.

"Pull over!" Raheim yelled. Pookie pulled over at a hotel near the highway.

"Get out! Now walk across the highway!" Raheim commanded the dude.

As the guy began to walk across the highway into on-coming traffic, cars began to swerve and honk trying to avoid him. He made it across two lanes before an 18-wheeler coming too fast to stop smashed into him throwing his now lifeless body across the freeway to the other side. More cars drove over him before it was all over. Pookie and Raheim slowly drove back home. Raheim had totally forgotten all about getting his precious unknowing bride-to-be's ring. Oh well, another day in the life of a thug.

They arrived back at the apartment. Before they could sit down good, it was already on the news about the death of the dude they were just with. Raheim broke out into laughter seeing his body fly through the air like a rag doll. Pookie, spooked at the thought that the scene was funny to Raheim, got up to leave.

"A'iight, I'm out. I'll hook up a meeting with KB next week." Pookie told Raheim.

"Yeah, man, Peace!" Raheim replied.

Did he just say 'Peace'? Pookie thought to himself. There was nothing peaceful about what just happened.

"Peace!" Pookie replied and thought he's getting worse. Maybe Bonquisha is the answer. She better get to him before it's too late.

# BUSINESS

"Yeah, man, so what's up? What you talkin' 'bout?" Raheim quizzed KB.

"I'm talking major weight, man. I can put you on the map beyond Miami." KB replied, hoping Raheim would bite. I just need to get in and it won't take long for me to take him down, thought KB. He's too careless and his game is whack.

"How I know you not 5-0? Who you runnin' wit'?" Raheim asked in between sips of his drink, Ciroc on the rocks with a splash of cranberry.

"Man, do I look like 5-0? I don't mess with them cats. They can't see me coming when I'm riding right beside them." KB reassured Raheim. "Besides, I got people working for me anyway. I just need the Miami connect to complete the circle." KB continued.

"Hold on, man! I ain't trying to join no other circle, I got my own thing working pretty good. Too many chiefs lead to some dead Indians, you feel me?" Raheim retorted.

"Your circle can't be bigger than what I'm working with! I'm talking, Pittsburgh, all of Jersey, Houston, even Hawaii! We stationed, ready to roll. All we need is you, Playa." KB tried to sound convincing.

Raheim's interest was peaked when KB said Hawaii. He had always wanted to go there. Maybe I do need to get with this cat he began to think. That'll be less work for me. Then I can really put more into Bonquisha and take the heat off of me.

"A'iight man, let's talk!" Raheim leaned in to get the details.

The music drowned them out as KB and Raheim talked, heads shaking in agreement, grinning from ear to ear thinking about all the money they were going to make. The waitress came over to offer any further beverages needed and KB ordered a bottle of champagne so they could celebrate the new collaboration.

Yes! I'm in! I knew that would be too easy, thought KB. Trying to contain his excitement, KB thought about his next moves to execute his plan. Raheim was going down and he didn't know it. This was truly a celebration indeed!

Sitting back in a more relaxed mode, Raheim thought to himself... This cat better not think he can play me. I am a lot smarter than he thinks. I know more people and my connections are better, but I'm going to play his game for a minute, make that paper...

"What up with you and Alexis? You got with that yet?" Raheim asked, switching gears.

"Yeah, man, thanks for that hook up. She is one fine lady." KB replied.

"One fine lady? You mean to tell me she's not a freak?" Raheim inquired.

"Nah man, she's not like that. That's not the kind of women I like anyway." KB replied.

"I know what you mean, man. That does get old... Sometimes you need something that's for real and not just about the money and sex. Too many of these broads have that 'what you gon' do for me' mentality... it's not worth it...not worth the trouble."

Raheim rambled on as he mentally reflected on his plans to be with Bonquisha.

By this time, KB had tuned out Raheim and was deep in his own thoughts about Alexis. How was he going to do this without hurting her? He was really beginning to fall for her, something an undercover should never do. There just has to be a way...

# GIRL TALK

"Okay, so spill the beans!!!! It must be good since you didn't even think about making it to church this morning….mhm hmm…." Bonquisha laughed while walking through my front door after banging on it so loud I am sure the neighbors are awake. That's all I need is for those bad kids to come running over like this is playtime or something.

"I…you know I wanted to go to church." I replied.

Bonquisha quickly cut me off, "Girl, PLEASE! You know you were all up under that man. Did you finally give in? Like, it's been almost five years!!!! I don't know how you manage…. couldn't be me! I gots ta' get mine…." Bonquisha laughed.

I was shocked but laughed right along with Bonquisha. She is too funny, but right! It has been a long time, but I refuse to let every man think he can have this. The right man is worth waiting for. I know one thing, he better be ready!

"Hellooo?!!!!!" Bonquisha yelled.

"What? Oh, I was in deep thought, sorry."

"Obviously!! Well, I'm waiting…what happened? How was it? What did you do? Come on, spit it out!" Bonquisha impatiently urged.

"So, he picked me up.."

"I know! I was here, remember??' Bonquisha interrupted.

"We went to Benny's of Miami."

"Ooohh, girl, I been wanting to go there!!! How was it?" Bonquisha asked.

"You know, if you interrupt me one more time! I am not going to tell the story." I replied as I crossed my arms and turned my head like an angry little girl.

"Okay, okay, no more interruptions, I promise." Bonquisha said.

I knew that was a promise she could not keep, I thought while laughing to myself. She cracks me up!

"We sat and ate dinner and talked and laughed and flirted all night. He ordered my favorite, Moscato. I had the salmon and salad. He had steak and shrimp.

The food was ever delightful, especially when he fed it to me. We talked more and cracked on each other back and forth. After eating, we danced a little. It seemed like the band had a list of all my favorite songs. After almost falling on my butt from the effects of the Moscato, we sat down to have dessert. Before I could even open my mouth, the waiter had chocolate covered strawberries, pineapples, and bite-sized chocolate cake pieces coming to the table along with more Moscato. Girl, I felt like if I had one more sip of Moscato, I was going to lose all my brownie points, Christian points, whatever points I thought I had." We laughed.

"So, what happened after that?" Bonquisha intensely inquired.

"We left. He took me home, walked me to the door and gave me a kiss on the cheek." I replied.

"On the cheek?!!! Are you serious?" Bonquisha shouted!

"Yes! He is a gentleman and he recognizes a real lady when he sees one!" I shot back.

"Whatever, that was lame as all the lame ducks in the pond!" Bonquisha laughed.

"Well, I didn't think so. Any man could have easily taken advantage of me in such a vulnerable state. He didn't and that really impressed me. Besides, he immediately called me and we talked until 4 am this morning. Hence, the reason I missed church this morning. So, how was church?"

"Not as good as this! You didn't miss anything. I was falling asleep and you know Sister Yarborough was nudging me and making faces at me. I just couldn't keep my eyes open and our awesome minister Brother Farquan wasn't making it any better with his boring sermon..." Bonquisha began when I interrupted her.

"Did you tell KB what I like? The Moscato, music, chocolate, even the place???? It all seemed too much like right." I asked.

"Girl, Please! When would I have had the time to tell him all that? If he is as smooth as you say he is, he probably figured it out on his own. You do talk all day everyday! I can't even get a phone call in between lately..."

"I know you not capping? You not trying to be jealous of my time are you???" I laughed.

"Ttt! You got me bent!" Bonquisha said while rolling her eyes.

"Awww, I miss you too! But you have to admit, this is the first time I have had any interaction with anybody other than you and it feels kind of nice to be on the other side of it for once. I'm the one always stuck listening to you and your stories."

"I know, I'm not tripping. I am truly happy for you, gurl!" We hugged. "Now, go brush your funky breath!" Bonquisha yelled.

"At least I wasn't all up in people face at church with it. You need a mint?" I laughed, although Bonquisha didn't seem too thrilled at my joke.

"What are we doing today?" She asked.

"I don't know. I have to check with my man...." I said smiling from ear to ear. She threw a pillow at me.

"You missed!" I screamed as I ran into the bathroom to freshen up.

"Yeah, well, I'll be out here when you get out!" She yelled back.

Yes, but I have water guns under the sink. Ready at all times!!!! What!?! I laughed to myself. I am truly in a happy place right now. I hope this is it!

# BLISS

I am totally engrossed in this guy. How did he come about and sweep me off my feet. He is such a gentleman. I hope he is not trying to dupe me. I can be a little gullible at times. Why do I feel like this for him? I wish my dad was here so I could talk to him. Maybe he is looking out for me up above....

There is nothing like watching the sun rise and having a nice cup of warm, flavorful coffee with so much cream and sugar it could be considered candy. There is so much negativity in the news and newspapers that all the sanity I have comes from enjoying this marvelous view from my huge kitchen bay window...and of course thinking of KB.

I shouldn't fall so deeply for him. You know, he does drive a Lamborghini, hangs around people like Raheim, has guns obviously.... hmmm. I need to do more investigation into him but he is so charming, such a gentleman, and very respectful. Where could you possibly find someone like him? Where did he come from? He is everything I am looking for in a mate. We talk all the time. It's like we can't seem to get enough time on the phone and when we are together, it's like we never want to leave each other's presence. I never once dreamed, okay, so I dreamed all the time of this happening and it now seems to be coming true. Is it too much for me to handle? Is this a trick? What if it's all not real? What if I get hurt?...Stop it, Stop it, Stop it!!! Just enjoy the moment. Live for each day as it comes. Don't rush yourself, your feelings, put them on pause!!!

I wonder how our kids would look? How they would act? Would they have more of his traits or mine? Would we have a boy or girl first or maybe even twins? Twins would be good, that way we can get it over with in one shot. I am so crazy!!! We haven't even gone there yet! But when we do, it is going to be off the chain! He is so fine, with just the most beautiful chocolate skin ever made. His hair is a soft curly black and he keeps it edged up real good....mmmm, yummy! This coffee is so good!

Alexis drifts into another world, her own little world, while finishing her coffee. It must be nice to not have to work but live wonderfully free and do whatever you want she thought to herself. Thinking about all of the volunteer organizations she has helped out and how she would not have been able to do that if it were not for how well her father had set her up. He always took care of Alexis. She was his world and nothing or no one could make him see any different. No one could even think about hurting Alexis without saying their last prayers. Alexis had it all and now was missing it all. Feeling alone in the world, until KB came along, Alexis was grateful for all she had.

Oh, look at the time! Let me stop all this daydreaming. I have to go save the world! Alexis said to herself. That's what her dad would say every morning and every time he kissed her forehead before leaving for work. 'I have to go save the world!' The more she thought about her father, the more she began to tear up. As the tears began to roll down her face, Alexis began to shake vigorously to help get herself together. 'Get it together, get it together', she told herself. 'Shake this off. My mother, daddy and God are watching over me,' she said, reassuring herself everything was going to be alright.

# MISTAKES

Man, I am making too many mistakes...letting too many boys in my business, Raheim thought to himself. This KB dude better check out or there's going to be hell to pay. Pookie is too close for comfort. I need to put some distance between me and him. The block is too hot since the shooting. These cops are not playing around and riding with Pookie is making me a target. Them cats don't know my vehicles, maybe it's time I start driving myself.... like I'm Miss Daisy or something...

Raheim laughed to himself at the thought of how he had everyone on edge and jumping at just the sight of him. His own cousin was his private chauffer whether he wanted the job or not. All his workers were scared of him from Miami to New York to all of Cali. This was the life...how it was supposed to be.

This is one crazy business but it more than pays the bills. It more than makes up for the struggle I had to endure as a child. No one should have to live like I did. That is why I do this...this is for my momma. Raheim thought to himself while smoking on a blunt. He had always said he wouldn't partake of his merchandise but being around it made it too hard to resist. It started with one puff here, one puff there, and before you know it he was doing it on a regular basis. One thing he didn't do and swore by his momma not to was smoke crack, snort cocaine, or shoot up heroin. That was totally out of the question. Once you start doing that, it's over! And Raheim knew it firsthand. His father got caught up and his family was never the same. Not Raheim! No way would he ever let things get to that level. There was too much at stake. He was working on building an empire, one that would last forever. Not one that would crumble because the crack, cocaine, and heroin knocked it down. Not one that was distraught because it was beating everyone in the house whether they did anything or not. Not one that sold everything that was worth anything just for that next moment of unaware pleasure, one moment of being eased of all pain and responsibility. That is not the life, the legacy, Raheim wanted to leave behind. The time had come. Raheim finally could see the light at the end of the tunnel. It was time to settle down. Make this one last big drop and move around. Marry Bonquisha, have

a few little Raheims, maybe one little Bonquisha.
Yep, it's time.

# HIDING

Keeping in all these feelings is driving me crazy. I have got to find a way to tell Alexis how much I love her. She is the light of my life and I want to make tonight special for her. All of this is making me lose focus. I knew better than to fall for her but I couldn't help it. The last time I met anyone like her, I let her get away. Not this time. But the betrayal of it all could end what we have. If my boss knew, he would remove me from the case and I could lose her for sure. I have got to figure out a way. Gotta call my granny. She will know what to do.

"Granny! How's it going?"

"Hey baby, Todd is that you?"

"No Granny, it's KB, your favorite grandson."

Granny started suffering from Dementia about a year ago. It started out slow but since I have been away in Miami it seems to have rapidly taken over. I didn't want to do it, but I had to put her in a home, especially while I was away. No one was going to take care of her like I do while I was gone. This place is supposed to be the best and it better be with all the money I am paying them.

"Oh, KB? You coming to see me today? I don't like it here. Your father came by. They gave me jello today."

My father? Granny was really losing it. My father was in a mental facility himself due to some bad drugs which is what propelled me into my career.

Well, I see this call is not going to be fruitful. I am going to have to figure this out for myself.

Granny continued to ramble on for another fifteen minutes before KB could get her off the phone. While she was talking, he was devising a plan to get Raheim out of hiding. Ever since he and Alexis met, Raheim has taken a backseat to everything. KB was hoping his cover hasn't been blown.

"Okay Granny. I have to go now. I love you."

"Okay baby, I love you too Todd."

KB hung up the phone saying a prayer for Granny. It hurt him to know she was in this condition and he couldn't be there. But, work had to get done and I was the best! Let me hit up Raheim right quick.

"Yo, Raheim, What up?"

"Ain't nuthin'...I can't call it. What up wit you?"

"Man, I was getting ready to roll through. Just got off the phone with my boys. They ready!"

"Oh yeah? Aight...roll on through."

They hung up the phone.

While KB was plotting and scheming, Raheim was constantly looking over his shoulder. Looking out the window, checking for surveillance cops hiding in plain sight, Raheim laughs to himself.

"What am I tripping for? They can't touch me with a ten-foot pole. I got this city on lock." Walking in circles, talking to himself, trying to pump himself up. It wasn't working. Raheim had this gut feeling and it had his nerves bad. That feeling is what has had him locked up in the house for two weeks, laying low. Pookie was running point on everything but Raheim made him park that loud color attention grabbing truck of his. Instead, he rented a silver Chevy Malibu. Pookie resisted at first, but understood that it was necessary to keep the business flowing.

With Pookie running things, Raheim could put more focus on setting up the new business and planning the proposal Bonquisha doesn't see coming but probably is expecting sooner or later.

Knock, Knock.

Frozen in thought as Raheim hears the knock at the door, he breaks his trance and reaches for his gun.

"Who is it!" Raheim shouts with a deep voice as if to sound fierce and dangerous. He had forgot that quick that KB was coming over.

"It's KB, Fool, open up!" KB shouted back.

"Man, don't be knocking on the door like you 5-0 or something."

KB laughed as he walked in to Raheim's house, surveying all of the cameras, weapons, and paraphernalia lying around. "I ain't no 5-0." KB shoots back. "What you so paranoid for anyway? Chill out dude. My set up is tight. You ain't got to worry 'bout me and mine," KB assures Raheim. "You acting like you killed a cop or something." KB jokes.

"Ey man, that ain't funny!" Raheim responds with a hint of seriousness in his tone.

"Oh, you did that?" KB asks, hoping to get the confession he needed.

"I done did a lot, dude! That's why I'm working to get out this game after this. The streets are too hot so this came along right on time." Raheim says.

"What you drinking?" He asks KB.

"Old Fashion." KB responds.

"Figures!" Raheim laughs.

"What?!" KB says, sounding offended.

"This cat I popped used to drink those all the time. He thought he was smooth. Always popping up on me trying to catch me in some action. One day, he got too smooth for his own good and I had to pop him. He was 5-0, the head in Miami." Raheim confessed.

Glad he had the recorder on him, KB replied, "Word? You serious in these streets. How you manage that and still alive nor got caught yet?"

"Like I said, I got Miami on lock." Raheim smirked while sipping his drink.

Not sure why he confessed, but KB was glad he did. That was all he needed to proceed forward with his plan. Alexis' dad was the head of Miami so, that's it right there. KB worked hard not to smile as he thought to himself, "Got 'em!". "What you say?" Raheim asked.

"Huh? Oh, nothing." KB finished his drink and then excused himself. "Gotta go get my girl and take her out. I just secured tickets to this concert she been wanting to go to and bugging me about all week. You know how it is…" KB laughs as he plays off almost getting caught. They dap it up and KB leaves.

Raheim has a strange feeling and weird thoughts come across his mind. "Nah! He wouldn't be that bold." He finishes his drink and then goes to bed.

# HURRY UP

"Always rushing me...geez. It takes time to get ready, to make this masterpiece"...Alexis thought as KB was sitting in the other room shouting out to her to Hurry Up!.

"I'm coming, I'm coming!" Alexis shouted back.

"We are going to be late. The show begins at 7 PM. It is 6 PM and we have almost an hour's drive to get there. All the good seats are going to be taken." KB shouts from the living room.

Rolling her eyes, Alexis is huffing and puffing while running around like a chicken with its head cut off. "Where was Bonquisha when you needed her. She knows I need help with hair, makeup, outfits, etc. I guess this will do. We are going to be outside anyway," she said to herself with one last look in the mirror.

"Alright, I am ready now." "It's about time. A man will starve to death waiting on you!" KB replied with a huge grin. He was looking Alexis up and down thinking of all of the things he could do to her but knew it would have to wait until marriage.

"I hope we make it that far." He said to himself but just loud enough that Alexis turned and asked what he said.

"Oh, nothing. Come on. Let's go." He recovered.

They were going on a date to the outdoor theater across town. A benefit concert with some of the latest stars was being put on in support of Change Across America. The idea was to bring awareness to the things going on around us and advocate for change for the better.

While driving, KB was lost in his thoughts and was quiet. Alexis broke the silence by turning the radio up loud and belting out the song on the radio. She couldn't really sing but gave it her best shot. KB looked at her like she was crazy and then joined in on the fun. He was a worse singer than she was, so that made them perfect for each other. They laughed as the song ended.

"So, Mr. Starving Man, what do you have packed in that picnic basket?" Alexis inquired.

"It's a surprise. You will like it, I promise." He assured her. She looked at him like she wasn't so sure with one eyebrow raised.

As they continued to drive, Alexis looked out of the window and began to daydream about their wedding day. KB hasn't proposed yet, but she knew he was going to soon. Their connection was so strong that it was inevitable. It was only a matter of time. "I know one thing for sure, he needs to hurry up." She thought to herself.

KB drifted into his own thoughts. "I need to hurry up and pull this off quick.

# MAKING MOVES

Alright. Time to stop playing with these fools. It's gon' be what it's gon' be. Now, if KB pulls this off, Imma be sitting FAT!!! Get me a yacht and chill with my lady soon to be wife...Raheim thought about what it would be like once this deal goes down. Man, to be running things from East Coast to West Coast all the way to the Pacific Ocean.... that's what's up!

Pookie picked up Raheim, still driving the rental even though he really missed being in his truck. The ladies he picked up along the way while riding in style was missed but Pookie had to lay low. It was the best thing for the business considering how hot things have been due to Raheim not being able to control his temper and killing that cop. If only Alexis knew it was him...

"Let's roll!," Raheim shouted as he got in the car interrupting Pookie's thoughts. "This better not be a set up neither!"

Pookie rolled his eyes. He was so tired of Raheim doubting him and treating him like he doesn't know how to make business deals. "This is the biggest deal ever and it can't go wrong. Gots to get mine so I can get from up under Raheim." All these thoughts ran through Pookie's head as he drove to the meeting spot.

"Man, that was the longest drive ever. For a while, something hasn't been feeling right, but I'm rolling with it. This thing goes through, you are going to be the next Kingpin of the world behind me!" Raheim declared to Pookie.

As they pulled up, two other cars were already parked. While getting out, a fourth car drove up. All the men in all the cars got out and stood in a circle, staring at each other and sizing each other up to see what they were about just by looking at their style of dress and the jewelry they each wore. The roaring sound of a Lamborghini could be heard not too far off in the distance. The circle broke so the yellow speed demon of a car could drive up between them.

"Flashy, attention needing, non-discreet buster!" Shouted Raheim. "But that is a tight ride. How much that set you back?"

KB hopped out, laughing, and shaking hands with everyone. This was the biggest deal of the century, of his lifetime. I better not mess this up he thought to himself. "Sup everybody! Man, that old thing? Not too much….cars like that cost nothing compared to the amount of paper we about to stack!"

Introductions were completed with everyone shaking hands, dapping it up, like some secret boy's club or fraternity. KB carefully laid out the plan with every ear at full attention. Everyone was in agreement and knew their part. With the meeting adjourned, all the players got in their vehicles and began their long trek home.

Pookie dropped Raheim off and then ventured into his own trouble. Raheim began planning how he was going to propose to Bonquisha. He checked the safe to marvel at the 3-karat diamond he purchased for her hoping it will fit her manly hands. "Man, that girl got some big hands…", he thought to himself.

There was a knock at the door interrupting his thoughts. Raheim grabs his gun and carefully looks out the window. "Ah, she's here…she's early… that's a first!"

Raheim proceeds to open the door after tucking away his gun. Bonquisha pushes through, as usual. She's always looking to catch someone there and ready for the fight that will no doubt ensue.

"Hey Poo Bear!" says Bonquisha as she leans in to kiss Raheim. He really hates that name but decides to kiss her anyway while rolling his eyes. She knows he hates it but does it anyway just to jack with him. She looks around and sees the rose petals everywhere and starts to get suspicious. Then she sees the table set for two with candles, wine, and a vase with 2 red roses in the middle.

"What is going on Poo Bear???" She screams with excitement in her voice.

Raheim kneels down and pull out the ring. He begins his speech about settling down and starting a family. Expressing his love for Bonquisha and his desire to make her his wife while fighting back tears. She never saw him like this before and knew he was serious.

Finally, he pops the question. "Bonquisha, will you marry me?"

"BOY, QUIT PLAYIN'!" she shouts as he slides the ring onto her finger. She flashed a huge smile, showing off her gold tooth.

They hugged for what felt like an eternity which was a first so she knew it was real. She kissed him passionately and he returned the favor. Backing up to the table while still kissing her, Raheim puts out the candles with his fingertips and pushes everything on the table to the floor. The food he ordered went cold...

# NOW'S MY CHANCE

After such a successful meeting, KB was in disbelief. His thoughts took over while he drove home. "This is it. I have to make my move before Raheim suspects anything. Things are getting tight. It's time to take out the trash, get rid of the vermin roaming freely about in these streets. These fools are so eager. They don't even see what's coming."

KB's plan played over in his head as the darkness started to turn to light. "Man, this is a long way home." He had to pick a spot that was far from everything so no one would be willing to try to follow him on his way to go meet with the task force. "Gotta make sure everything is in place. One wrong move can blow this whole thing. The deal is supposed to go down in two days. It's all or nothing!! Once this is over, I can hopefully breathe for a minute. In the meantime, I need to work on sealing the deal with Alexis." His thoughts continued.

Finally arriving home, KB jumps in the shower. Checking his voicemail, he realizes he missed a call from Alexis. He almost forgot about the date he planned. Something real special was in store for his special lady. She was truly a gem and he couldn't risk losing her. Smiling while getting dressed and checking the mirror one last time before leaving, KB realized he hadn't slept any...oh well! No rest for the weary; but it's all good, especially when it is for a good cause.

KB could not stop smiling. Everything was going right. Even the little bad kids in Alexis' neighborhood couldn't make him feel anything other than happiness. Walking to the door with a dozen roses and assorted flowers in hand, Alexis wastes no time opening the door to let him inside. Smiling from ear to ear as well, she takes the flowers and smells them. After taking in the scents, Alexis looks beyond the flowers and proceeds to lean in to give KB a kiss. Anxiously waiting, he pulls her close, almost smushing the flowers. In the background, they hear the sounds of kids saying 'ooohhhhh.... naaasssty....they kissin'", while running down the street back to their own home. Neither of them was deterred from the moment. Now with lipstick all over his face, KB asks if Alexis is ready.

"Absolutely. Where you taking me today?" Alexis replies.

"It is a surprise." He retorts

"You and your surprises!" she says.

They arrive at the Italian restaurant which KB bought out just for this occasion. Red carpet was rolled out and covered with rose petals leading into the restaurant. As they entered the restaurant, the band immediately started playing soft slow tunes. One lone table sat in the middle of the restaurant with a bouquet of roses as the centerpiece. Candles lit up the restaurant for a fully romantic affair.

In her mind, Alexis was practically coming out of her clothes. She knew at this moment that this was the man she wanted to give herself to forever. Just before sitting down, KB spun Alexis around and as she came out of the spin to face him, she found him on his knee with a big cheesy grin and a small box in his hand. Covering her face with her hands out of excitement, she fought hard to hold back her tears to prevent messing up her makeup.

KB grabs her hand and begins to profess his love for Alexis. He opens the box to a shiny 5-karat diamond ring with platinum band. It was shining so brightly that she started screaming.

"Alexis, will you marry me?" KB asks.

"YES!!! YES!!! YES!!!" Alexis screams while jumping up and down. She was so loud the band briefly stopped playing.

KB slides the ring onto her finger and she stares at it in disbelief. This was the best day of both of their lives.

# BUILD UP

"You ready?" Raheim asks Pookie. Pookie is nervous but excited all at the same time. He gives Raheim a look of confidence although he is experiencing turmoil inside. If this deal goes sour, Pookie knows he is as good as dead, cousin or not.

"I was born ready!" Pookie shouts back over the music. Anytime something big is about to go down, Raheim has to blast music like it is the end of the world. "Thank goodness it is loud so he can't hear my heart beating," Pookie thought to himself not realizing he actually said it out loud.

"What you say?!" Raheim shouted.

"Man, turn that durn music down…maybe you can hear me!" Pookie responded with a big cheesy smile so as not to ignite Raheim's temper by his smart remark.

All the other team members were arriving one by one.

"Did ya'll park around back?" Raheim drills them. They all give a big nod and respond "YEAH", sounding like an echo in a mountain range. They continue to prepare for the deal, packaging product and money to make for the smooth transition. Guns are loaded and tucked, ready for whatever.

Across town, KB was prepping the team for what was to come. They are hovered over a table looking at a map. KB points out the areas where each team will be posted, bullet proof vests on and guns ready. Everyone is nodding their heads acknowledging their understanding of the task at hand. They know this is really big and could land them all a promotion along with a hefty reward, if they survive. Their hearts are beating fast as they take deep breaths to calm themselves down. A steady hand is required in these high intense situations. They load up in their vehicles and begin to head out.

KB stays back a bit so there is some distance and to say a little prayer.

# The Warning

Bonquisha comes barging through the front door. She is out of breath, bent over with her hand to her chest. Raheim is looking at her wondering what the heck is wrong with her. As she catches her breath, she stares Pookie down with the meanest mean mug anyone could give. Now Raheim is looking back and forth at Pookie, then Bonquisha. The hairs on the back of his neck begin to stand at attention. When this happens, Raheim knows something is about to go wrong.

She was trying to catch her breath, because she literally ran all the way there. Why? Who knows, but it must be really important because running is not in her vocabulary. A strange feeling begins to come over Raheim. He retrieves a glass of water and hands it to Bonquisha. She gulps it down like it is her last meal. Finally able to stand at attention, followed by one big sigh, a hard roll of the eyes, and a turn of her back to Pookie swinging her weave in the process, she begins to rattle off at the mouth. She is talking so fast Raheim is not able to understand what she is saying.

"Slow down!!!" he yells at her.

"Man, you will not believe what I just found out!!!" she shouts. "I was down the street on the corner talking to Rasheeda. And, she told me that her boyfriend cousin heard that some new cat in town was out to get you." She said with her arms folded across her chest.

"Who me?" Raheim pointed at himself.

"YES, YOU!" Bonquisha replied.

"This bet' not be who I think it is!" Raheim shouted while giving Pookie the stank eye. He began pacing in circles and started talking to himself. Pookie knew when Raheim did this, it wasn't good and began to get nervous.

"She said something about a Kenneth Bowman." Bonquisha continued. Everyone laughed.

"Kenneth Bowman? What kind of name is that?" Raheim retorted. "I would go by KB too if I was named Kenneth Bowman." Laughter continues to erupt when a loud knock interrupted the fun.

Raheim grabbed Bonquisha and kissed her tightly. He told her he loved her and hit her on the butt as he pushed her away. "Get out of here now and go to our hideout." he told her.

"Pookie, get the door!" Raheim shouted. He wanted Pookie to get shot first for setting him up, the ultimate betrayal.

KB enters the room. Everyone is on edge but remaining calm as if they were not aware of the situation at hand.

"What up?" Raheim asked KB as they exchanged handshakes and such. KB could sense something wasn't right but played it off as best he could. He knew this was risky, comes with the job.

"Can't call it." KB replied. "You ready to do this?" he asked Raheim while taking an assessment of the room.

"Yeah man, beyond ready!" Raheim responds, not giving away the fact that he knows what's about to go down.

Both KB and Raheim were in deep thought about the women they love and how today's outcome is going to impact them. They can only hope for the best. But as always, they are prepared for the worst.

Breaking the train of thought, KB begins to set the plan in motion.

"My contact is outside now. After this, we will be set for life. No worries about anything. Not about who we killed, not about cops, no longer looking over our shoulder. This is going to be it, dude!" KB says as he opens the door.

# DISCOVERY

"POOKIE!!!! I told you this man was not legit! How you jus' gon' bring 5-0 up in my camp!! Are you crazy?!! Knew I shouldn't have trusted you!" Raheim shouted while spraying bullets out of the window firing back at the cops.

"MAN!! I swear I didn't know! I really thought he was legit!" Pookie responded.

"That is why your main job was to drive me around. I knew what I was doing!" Raheim shouts back. Pookie rolls his eyes.

The sound of guns firing bullets continued to ring out loud throughout the neighborhood as Raheim and his team were in a huge battle with the cops. KB took a few of his men and ran around the back of the house while the rest of the cops kept shooting from the front. Bonquisha got popped and fell to the ground trying to make her escape. Raheim's men were dropping like flies as they were caught off guard.

At the end of the shootout, Raheim fell dead, Pookie was arrested, and Bonquisha was taken to the hospital with several injuries and a broken heart. The captain congratulated KB on a job well done.

Checking himself for injuries, KB jumped in his car and headed over to Alexis' house. He wanted her to hear it from him instead of the 5 o'clock news.

Boom! Boom! Boom!

"Who's this knocking on my door now like it's the end of the world?! It better not be those darn kids again. I know that much! I am so tired of them and their parents' drama! UGH!!!..." Alexis shouted. She began to become more and more irritated as she walked toward the door, bat in hand just in case.

As she looked through the peephole, her heart began to pump faster and faster at the site on the other end. She proceeded to unlock and open the door. KB barged in with blood all over his shirt. Immediately, she began to check his vitals, panicking at the thought of him being hurt, reminiscing on what she went through with her father. This was not something Alexis was ready to face again. It started to seem like death just keeps finding her.

Her thoughts were interrupted when KB grabbed her, embraced her tightly and began planting deep passionate kisses on her. She forgot all about the blood-soaked shirt that he still had on and kissed him back just as passionately.

He began to tell her what happened and why he was really in town. As the story unfolded, Alexis was both saddened and overjoyed. Finally, she received justice for her father's cold-blooded murder. It was so undeserved. She knows he is able to rest now.

"We got 'em! We got 'em!" KB was shouting, interrupting her thoughts as she took in all he was saying.

"Thank goodness! But how did you get all this blood on you?" Alexis inquired.

KB paced in circles with his hand over his mouth. "The shooting slowed. I was standing in the backyard surveying the dead. Raheim came running out the back door. He had been shot multiple times. As I turned around, he collapsed in my arms, looked me in my eyes and took his last breath."

"Oh wow!" Alexis replied in disbelief. "That had to be creepy."

"No, it comes with the territory." KB stated. "Now, let me go get cleaned up and submit my report at the office. I will be back in a couple of hours to take you out."

"Okay." That was all she could say. Still in shock and overcome with emotion, she kissed KB goodbye and closed the door behind him.

As promised, KB returned and whisked her away. They went to the bistro nearby. He ate as if it was his last meal....I guess he worked up an appetite Alexis thought to herself while playing with her salad.

# DECISIONS

Waking up after the most peaceful sleep she had in a long time, Alexis yawned and stretched while climbing out of the bed. "Man, that was some good sleep! I almost want to climb back in bed for a couple more hours!" Shaking out her legs as she walked to the bathroom. A nice hot shower, wash of the hair, squeaky clean teeth and fresh breath, she was now ready to take on the world.

Although she did feel relief, she also felt different. No more phone ringing to wake her up and hear all of the juicy details from her bestie! She shrugs her shoulders and heads to the kitchen. "Ahhh, nothing like the smell of coffee!" she says to herself.

Alexis had some decisions to make. Her thoughts flooded her mind... "I can't believe he looked at me with surprise. He didn't know my strength. He should have known since he knew my father. But I can't talk. I should have known what he was up to this entire time. Something didn't feel right but I ignored it. Could you blame me? I mean, dude is fine! And this beautiful ring ain't too bad either!!! He certainly pulled the wool over my eyes. He was smooth. Had everyone fooled. But I'm glad he did it. Those evil people needed to pay for killing my father. He was a good man and did a lot for the community. I feel bad for Bonquisha though. Just when it seemed like things were taking a positive turn for her, this happens. I tried to tell her Raheim was no good for her and she deserved better. She's so stubborn; won't listen for nuthin'! Now look at her, all bruised and broken, shot in the shoulder, concussion, leg in a cast. At least she survived, but at what cost? Was it really worth it? Only she can answer that question. Will our friendship last since I am with the guy who killed her man? Well, she was with the guy who killed my father....hmmm"

Alexis took a sip of her coffee and continued in her thoughts. "What I am afraid of is Pookie. He went crazy once he found out who KB really is. Now I hear he is in prison plotting for revenge. He has a few of his boys on the outside that survived the ordeal and got away. They are ready to jump when he gives the word."

As she poured her second cup of joe, which was very unusual for her to have more than one cup a day, Alexis drifted into her fairytale mindset. "I am not sure about my future with KB because of this. Staying with him puts my life in jeopardy. But these fools are not crazy. They know they bet' not mess with me. All of Miami police will come down on them so hard and no one will come out alive. They all promised my father they would take care of me."

Alexis finishes her coffee. She grabs a bagel and applies a hefty amount of strawberry cream cheese on it and an apple. "I'm supposed to be meeting with KB today. He wants to talk to me about everything, fill me in on the details such as how he really knew my father, how he found me, etc. We need to discuss our future too. Guess I better get ready." Still daydreaming as she proceeds to her bedroom to get ready to meet KB, the love of her life.

# OUTCOME

Well, after all of that, Alexis forgave KB. How could she not? He did bring down the man who killed her father. She honestly cannot believe it was Raheim. For him to look her in the eyes after all this time knowing what he had done is like sending a spear through her heart. It is like he was laughing in Alexis' face the entire time.

Bonquisha is caught up in all of this. She had to have known. How could she not since she was right there under him the whole time? Inquiring minds wonder if she kept Alexis close because she knew.

Well, none of that matters now. Alexis is smiling while walking down the aisle. Truly she was wishing her father was there physically by her side. Fighting back tears while thinking of her father and the fact that her best friend could not be there. As she sees KB's huge grin, looking like a kid in a candy store, Alexis forgets all about her troubles.

KB did catch flack from his captain for falling in love with Alexis as that was not part of the plan. However, Captain couldn't help but see they were made for each other. He hated to lose KB to Miami as he signed the transfer papers for KB's relocation. At least Captain knew he would still be able to call on KB when needed.

Bonquisha did show up to the wedding, however, Alexis was unaware. She hid in the upstairs waiting room out of site, but in plain view. While happy for Alexis to finally get her prince, Bonquisha was plotting her revenge. "Be happy for now, my friend. Be happy for now." Bonquisha said to herself.

Pookie was in prison for 10 years for his role in the entire ordeal. His goons on the outside are sitting, waiting….

Made in the USA
Columbia, SC
02 February 2025

53105608R00065